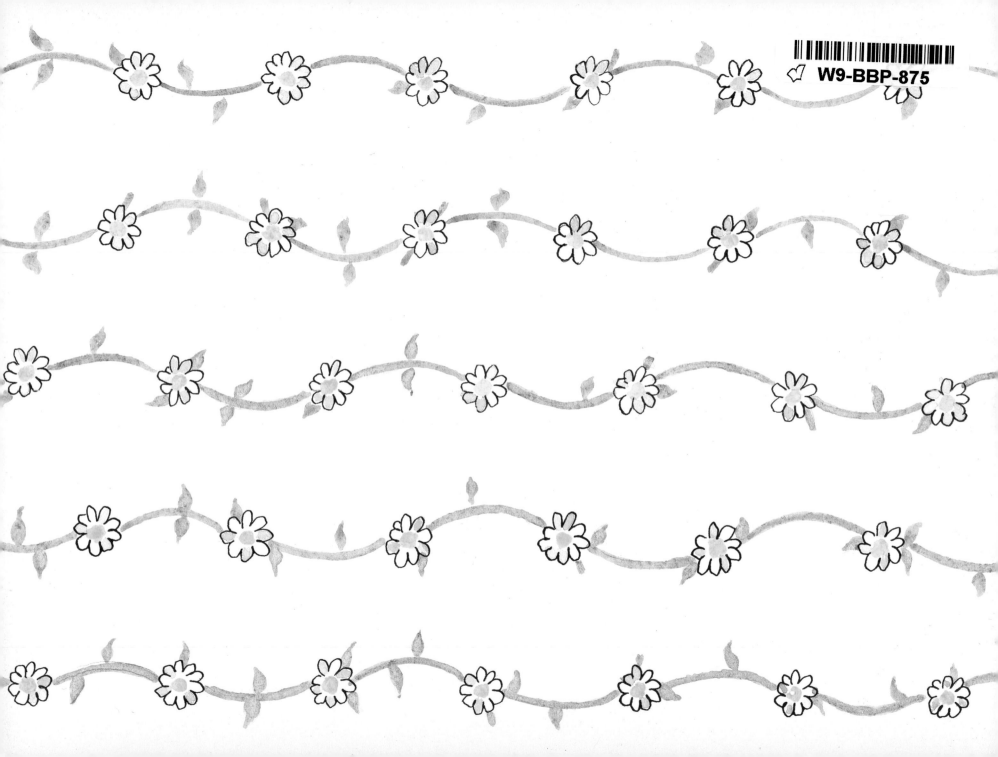

To Daisy and Rosie – love Mij

For Alison – Nicholas

tiger tales
an imprint of ME Media, LLC
5 River Road, Suite 128, Wilton, CT 06897
Published in the United States 2012
Originally published in Great Britain 2011
by Hodder Children's Books
a division of Hachette Children's Books
Text copyright © 2011 Mij Kelly
Illustrations copyright © 2011 Nicholas Allan
WKT0511
ISBN-13: 978-1-58925-107-6
ISBN-10: 1-58925-107-5
Printed in China
All rights reserved
1 3 5 7 9 10 8 6 4 2

For more insight and activities,
visit us at www.tigertalesbooks.com

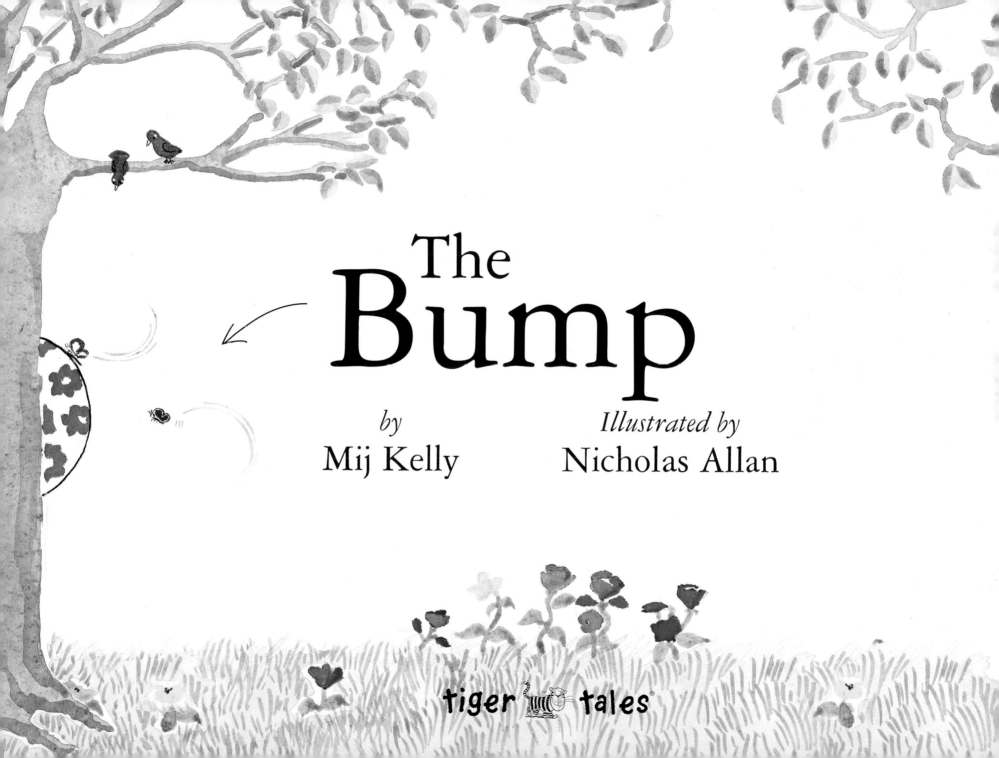

The
Bump

by
Mij Kelly

Illustrated by
Nicholas Allan

tiger tales

This is a story about someone you know
and something that happened a few years ago,
before she was famous for loving you
and for hip-hip-hooraying the things that you do
and mopping your spills and kissing you better. . . .

It's about your mommy before you met her.

The story begins on the day her world changed.
She felt a bit sick and a little bit strange.

Then, all of a sudden, her heart gave a thump,
when she looked in the mirror and noticed a bump.

Well, maybe she felt a little bit scared,
very excited and not quite prepared,

but right then and there she whispered, "Hello,"
and felt her love begin to grow.

Then out she went into the sun
to show the bump to everyone,

and dress it up in daisy chains
and think of extra-special names . . .
for the bump.

She treasured the bump like she treasures you,
and the bump – like her love – grew and grew.

It grew and grew like anything,
until her buttons all went . . . PING!

So she bought a humongous tent to wear,
a flowery tent for the bump to share,

NEW!

Peppermint
&
Onion

Ice cream!

and ate apples and peaches and other good things
(plus green ice cream and onion rings) . . . for the bump.

She looked after the bump
like she looks after you,
and the bump – like her love –
grew and grew.

It grew so very big and stout
that games of hide-and-seek
were out!

She showed her doctor her marvelous bump
and heard its heart going **thumpety-thump** . . .

and saw the baby hiding inside
and laughed out loud and almost cried.

The picture they gave her exists today –
she kept it safely tucked away.

She cherished that bump like she cherishes you,
and the bump – like her love – grew and grew.

It grew to such a stupendous size
that she accidentally won a prize!

She hugged it and lugged it all across town.
She never once stopped and put that bump down,
but rushed around in search of things
like stripy socks and teething rings
and bibs and hats and itsy mitts . . .

she even tried to learn to knit.

She cared for the bump like she cares for you,
and the bump – like her love – grew and grew.

It grew till the baby curled up inside
was suddenly far too big to hide.

This is a story of someone you know
and something that happened a few years ago.

It happened the day the baby unfurled
and came out of the bump and into the world.

And maybe you felt a little bit scared,
very excited and not quite prepared . . .

but there was your mommy saying, "Hello!"
with a love for you that grows and grows.

And now you're walking on your own.
Just look how big her love has **grown!**